BARBARA KER WILSON was born and brought up in north-east England. She began her publishing career as a children's editor with Oxford University Press and went on to be a managing editor at The Bodley Head and William Collins. In Australia she has worked as a managing editor with a number of publishers, and in 2000 she received the Dromkeen Medal for contributions to Australian children's literature. She has written over 40 books for adults and children. Her other books for Frances Lincoln are *The Turtle and the Island* and *Maui and the Big Fish*.

MEILO SO was born in Hong Kong and first came to the United Kingdom in 1979 to complete her education. She studied art in Oxford and Brighton before returning to Hong Kong to embark upon a career as a freelance illustrator. She is now a part-time illustrator with many magazine credits to her name. Her other book for Frances Lincoln is *The Monkey and the Panda*.

For Max – B.K.W.

For R.McS., R.D.I. – M.S.

Wishbones copyright © Frances Lincoln Limited 1993
Text copyright © Barbara Ker Wilson 1993
Illustrations copyright © Meilo So 1993

First published in Great Britain in 1993 by
Frances Lincoln Children's Books, 4 Torriano Mews,
Torriano Avenue, London NW5 2RZ
www.franceslincoln.com

This edition published in Great Britain and the USA in 2009

British Library Cataloguing in Publication Data available on request

ISBN 978-1-84507-938-3

Printed in China

9 8 7 6 5 4 3 2 1

Wishbones

A folk tale from China

RETOLD BY BARBARA KER WILSON • ILLUSTRATED BY MEILO SO

FRANCES LINCOLN
CHILDREN'S BOOKS

Thousands of years ago, in a cave among the hills of China south of the clouds, there lived a chieftain called Wu. Wu's first wife had died, leaving a daughter called Yeh Hsien. Her father loved her dearly.

But Wu's second wife, who had a daughter of her own, was unkind to her stepdaughter. Every day she forced Yeh Hsien to chop wood, and sent her to draw water from deep wells in dangerous places.

One day, while drawing water from a mountain pool,
Yeh Hsien saw a small fish with red fins and golden eyes.
Such a fish has never been seen before or since.

  Yeh Hsien caught the fish, brought it home to the cave
and put it in a bowl of water. She fed it on grains of rice
saved from her own plate.

Each day, the fish grew larger and larger until at last it was too big for the bowl, and Yeh Hsien moved it into the pond that lay close by the cave.

Whenever she went to the pond, the huge fish would rise to the surface and pillow its head on the bank. But it would appear only for Yeh Hsien, never for anyone else.

"I should like to see that fish!" Yeh Hsien's stepmother said to her own daughter one day. "I have often waited by the pond, but it will never appear for me."

Then the stepmother thought of a cunning trick. That night, when Yeh Hsien came home tired from her hard day's work, her stepmother said: "Poor Yeh Hsien! How shabby you look in your worn-out coat. Take it off. Let me lend you my beautiful new jacket."

Yeh Hsien was astonished, but she did as she was told and put on the jacket. It felt warm and comfortable after her threadbare old coat.

The next day, Yeh Hsien was sent off on a long journey into the hills to gather herbs. As soon as she was out of sight, her stepmother put on Yeh Hsien's old coat, and hid a sharp knife up her sleeve. "Now we will see that precious red and golden fish," she told her daughter.

She went to the pond and called to the fish. The fish, believing it was Yeh Hsien standing there, leapt from the water and laid its head on the bank. Immediately the cunning stepmother killed it with her sharp knife. Then she took it back to the cave and cooked it for their supper.

"This is the best fish I have ever tasted," Wu said, smacking his lips. His wife smiled. She did not tell her husband that it was Yeh Hsien's fish. After supper, she buried the fishbones in the dunghill outside the cave.

Imagine Yeh Hsien's sorrow when she returned to discover her fish had gone! She went to the pond and called, but in vain.

As she stood weeping, an old man with unkempt hair and a ragged coat appeared as if from the sky and stood before her.

"Don't cry, Yeh Hsien. Your stepmother killed the fish and buried its bones in the dunghill. But those bones are magic. Hide them, and whatever you wish for will be granted."

Yeh Hsien did as she was told and she found, just as the old man had said, that she could have anything she wanted by wishing on the fishbones. Before long she had jewels, finely-carved jade and embroidered silk robes hidden away in her corner of the cave.

Soon it was Cave Festival time, when the people of the hills south of the clouds gathered to celebrate and make music. Wu, Yeh Hsien's stepmother and her stepsister set out to join the feasting, but Yeh Hsien was left to guard the fruit orchard behind the caves. Her father was sorry to leave her, but he did not dare to say anything for fear of his wife.

Yeh Hsien longed to go to the Cave Festival. No sooner was her family out of sight than she took off her everyday clothes and dressed herself in a shining blue and purple robe, with violet silken slippers upon her small feet. All these the magic fishbones had brought her. Then she set out for the Festival.

How Yeh Hsien enjoyed herself! She ate sweet bean cakes, laughed and listened to the music, tapping her feet in their new violet slippers, and was dazzled by the lights of a hundred lanterns.

Later, as her eyes became used to the lights, she glanced about, and saw her stepmother and stepsister looking at her in a puzzled way. Perhaps they recognised her!

Seeing their frowns, Yeh Hsien grew frightened and ran away and, as she fled, a silken slipper fell from her foot.

When her stepmother came home, she found Yeh Hsien asleep beneath a mulberry tree, wearing her everyday clothes once more. "How could I have imagined that the beautiful woman in the blue and purple robe at the Festival was my wretched stepdaughter?" she asked herself.

Now, not far from that place lay the Kingdom of T'o Huan. After the Festival, the cave people found Yeh Hsien's violet slipper and took it to the King of T'o Huan, who at once bought the precious object.

The young king commanded all the women of his household
to try on the slipper, but it proved too small for even the
tiniest foot.

"I will find the lotus-footed lady to whom this slipper belongs!" the king declared. "She shall be my queen!" He sent out messengers with the precious slipper to search the countryside.

At last they came to Wu's cave. First Yeh Hsien's stepmother tried on the slipper: it was far too small for her. Next her daughter thrust it on her foot, but it was too small for her too. Last of all, Yeh Hsien tried the slipper. It fitted her tiny foot perfectly.

While her stepmother and stepsister watched in astonishment, Yeh Hsien ran to her corner of the cave and put on the matching violet slipper and her fine blue and purple robe. Then the messengers took her back to the young King of T'o Huan, who made her his wife and queen of all the land.

And what happened to those magic fishbones, Yeh Hsien's wonderful wishbones? She took them with her to T'o Huan, but the king wished for so much jade and jewellery and silk and gold during the first year of their marriage, that at last the fishbones refused to grant any more of his desires.

"Husband, you have worn out their magic," Yeh Hsien gently chided him.

The king was deeply ashamed. He buried the fishbones near the sea-shore and later the tide washed them away. They have never been found to this day.

MORE PAPERBACKS FROM FRANCES LINCOLN CHILDREN'S BOOKS

THE TURTLE AND THE ISLAND
Barbara Ker Wilson
Illustrated by Frané Lessac

A traditional folk tale describing how the great sea turtle builds
the island of Papua New Guinea, and finds a wife and home
for a lonely man in a dark cave, far beneath the waves.

MAUI AND THE BIG FISH
Barbara Ker Wilson
Illustrated by Frané Lessac

Long ago when the world was new and little Maui
was born, the great god Tama carried him away to the underworld
to learn magic. When Maui came back, his brothers made fun of him
and wouldn't take him deep-sea fishing. They stole away on a fishing trip,
thinking he was still asleep… How Maui outwitted his brothers, caught
the biggest fish in the ocean and became Maui of the Thousand Tricks
is vividly retold in this traditional Polynesian folk tale.

THE MONKEY AND THE PANDA
Antonia Barber
Illustrated by Meilo So

Lean, lively Monkey plays naughty tricks and makes the
village children laugh. But in their quieter moments the children prefer
the company of fat, friendly Panda. Which is more lovable, the Monkey or the Panda?
Antonia Barber's story of the contest between the animals, accompanied by
Meilo So's striking images, combines allegory with fun
in this enchanting oriental tale.

Frances Lincoln titles are available from all good bookshops.
You can also buy books and find out more about your favourite titles,
authors and illustrators on our website: www.franceslincoln.com